Ali Bahrampour

Abrams Books for Young Readers • New York

For Nava and Giev

The illustrations in this book were made with pen and ink and watercolor.

Cataloging-in-Publication Data has been applied for and may be
obtained from the Library of Congress.

ISBN 978-1-4197-4571-3

Book design by Steph Stilwell

Printed and bound in China
10 9 8 7 6 5 4 3 2 1

ABRAMS The Art of Books
195 Broadway, New York, NY 10007
abramsbooks.com

Bobo was home rolling around in the mud
when somebody slipped a letter under the door.

It was an invitation to have dinner with the queen.

"Why me?" Bobo wondered.

He was a lone boar who kept to himself in the forest;
he was covered in fleas.

The letter said a car would come pick him up in the morning.

That night Bobo had a hard time falling asleep,
and not just because of his fleas.

How would he know which fork to use?

Could he pick up a glass with his hooves?

The car woke him up. He had overslept!

The drive to the palace took most of the day.

“It’s a dinner to celebrate the new queen!” said one of the passengers.

“They say no one’s ever seen her!” said another.

“I hope there’s food,” said Bobo.

“Is anyone else itchy?” asked the man sitting next to Bobo.

The wild pig had never seen anything so grand.

He couldn't believe he had been invited.

Neither could the palace guards.

"I guess I should have worn clothes," Bobo thought.
He looked around for something to slip into.

This wasn't it.

As servants cleaned up Bobo's mess,
it was announced that dinner would be served in an hour.

"That's a long time to wait," thought the boar.

Bobo was happy to see he wasn't the only one underdressed.

Just then his fleas got a burst of energy.

"That's it!" said the guards. "Throw him out."

“I’m not leaving before dinner!” Bobo yelled.

He had to find someplace he wouldn’t be seen.

This wasn't it.

But he was able to slip out in the confusion.

"Here's a place a boar can hide," thought Bobo.

But just then a flea crawled up his nose . . .

. . . and he sneezed.

Bobo hot-hoofed it down the hallway.

What luck!
Nobody would mind if he had a little snack.

But a stray pat of butter had other plans.

"How strange life can be," Bobo thought.

Bobo found himself taking a shortcut to dinner.

He arrived just as they were bringing in the queen.

“WHO MADE THIS MESS?”
screamed a voice from inside the royal box.

There was total silence.

Nobody moved.

“It was me, Your Highness,”
Bobo confessed.

“WELL DONE!”
squealed the queen.

The people went wild, thrilled that they could finally have some fun.

Yodeling with joy, they carried out the boars in triumph.

Bobo and the queen, meanwhile, were really hitting it off. To celebrate their newfound friendship, they decided to throw an even bigger party in the woods.

“We’ll invite everyone!” said Bobo.

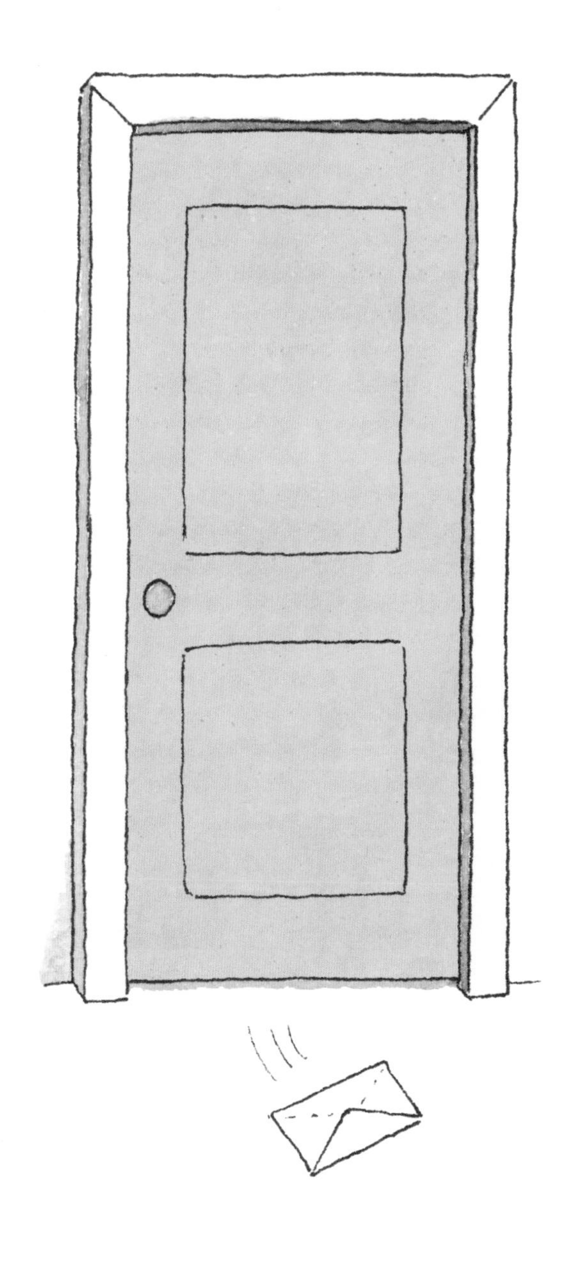

So keep an eye out.